Life of a Terrarian

Aiden Barger

Contact the author

https://www.AidenBarger.com

Word Count: 21,104

Editor: Kelly Barger

ISBN-13: 978-0-578-76206-7 (paperback)

First Edition

0, 1, 1, 2, 3, 5, 8, 13, 21, 34, 55, 89, 144, …

"Who dares wins."

British Special Air Service

1

A New Life

When I first entered the Terraria world, I had no idea where I should even begin. I started by reviewing my supplies to see what I had. I had an axe, a wooden one at least. I also had a semi-broken pickaxe and a sword. After reviewing my supplies, I looked up and saw a guy standing nearby. I wondered if maybe he could help me so I walked over to him.

"Hey, I'm new here. What should I do?"

"I'm the guide. If you want to know what to do next, you should build a house for me."

Build a house? I didn't have a clue what I needed to do that. I thought about it, and I guessed the logical first step was to chop a few trees for wood. I found it to be really easy to chop trees. I didn't know why, but I had expected it to be difficult.

After I had cut my thirteenth tree, I decided to

start building a house. I put in the floor, which was nice looking wood. I took a quick break and then decided to build a chair. Table. Crafting bench. Done, done and done. Then I built the walls and the roof. Oh, a door, I nearly forgot the door! After so much work, I planned to rest for the night and start again the next morning.

Morning arrived, and I wondered what I should do next? Hmm. I knew! I went out to ask the guide for further details.

"Good morning. I've built you a house. What should I do now?"

"Go kill a slime to make a torch. It will make exploring the world easier. While you're at it, craft a set of wooden or cactus armor," the guide said.

Okay. That was good information. I immediately started hunting a slime. I remembered a green blob thing that passed by my house while I was building. I decided to track it down. Yay! I spotted it right away. Oh! It was coming toward me, and it looked like it was going to attack. That must be why I had a sword to defend myself. I hit the green slime with my sword and pushed it back. It started shaking and I didn't know why, but it jumped at me again! The second time it had more energy. Ouch! That really hurt! I kept striking the green slime with my sword. It took a while to kill the green slime, but I finally did. It dropped some gel, which I picked up to add to my supplies. After that battle, I headed back home. When I returned, I discovered the guide had moved into my house. It looked like I would need to build more houses.

Wow! I seemed to be getting the hang of building because I quickly completed two more houses. Then I remembered what the guide had said about the torch. I played around with the crafting bench to see what I could make. One wood and the gel from the green slime made three torches, which would come in really handy! I decided to go out to explore a bit. I had seen a cave nearby so I wanted to check it out, and exploring the cave would give me a chance to try out my new torch.

Wow! The cave was dark and creepy and filled with stone. I spotted something in the dirt, but I needed my pickaxe to break it. Hmm. It was interesting. A heart-shaped crystal. It disappeared in my hand, and I immediately felt healthier. I decided the heart crystals must be really good for me. I saw a few more and decided to collect them, too.

I noticed a pink thing over in the corner of the cave. Upon closer inspection, it was a pinky slime! I hit it with my sword, and it attacked me ferociously. After a long battle, I killed the pinky slime and picked up pink gel and a gold coin. I explored the cave for a while longer and killed one more pinky slime. When it was time to rest, I traveled back home to get some sleep.

I couldn't believe it was morning already. I heard a noise and looked out the door. There was a merchant and a nurse moving into my houses. I didn't know why they were coming into the houses I had built. I wondered if they had decided to visit. I smiled and felt like I was doing a great job. I was making friends, I had extra supplies, and I already had two gold coins. I thought my new Terraria life was going to be easy!

I wondered what I should next, and I decided to explore more of the world to understand what I was up against. I saw mostly green slimes as I traveled, but I finally spotted a blue slime. I moved closer to fight it to see what it would give me.

Whew! That blue slime was much harder to fight than the green slime, and it hurt more. With several good whacks with my sword, I finally killed it. I got the same number of gel as the green slime and added the gel to my supplies for later. After my successful battle against the blue slime, I kept walking. I had been walking for a while and was getting a little bored when I looked up and spotted a huge tree!

2

Enchanted Boomerang

The huge tree was hollow so I decided to look inside.
There were many chests with weird items in them. One
was an enchanted boomerang, which did fourteen damage.
I was excited to have found such an amazing weapon, but
I decided I better not waste any more time and get to my
to do list. Crafting some armor like the guide suggested
was next on my list. He said I should craft cactus or
wooden armor so I headed back to my house to use the
crafting bench.

Bam! I had a wooden armor set in no time. I tried
it on and practiced with the enchanted boomerang. It was
hard to control, but I finally got the hang of it. If I aimed
the boomerang correctly, I could kill six slimes in one
deadly shot! It was getting boring just fighting slimes so I
headed toward the jungle to find more powerful enemies.

I reached the jungle and discovered it had enemies

that were very difficult to fight. I chopped some of the jungle's mahogany trees to see if their wood would make better armor. My plain wooden armor just wasn't cutting it because it allowed me to take too much damage. To stay safe and not worry about being killed, I enclosed myself in a little square made of dirt blocks. I placed a mahogany crafting bench and crafted my new armor. I put on the mahogany armor and left the safety of my dirt square to fight an enemy and see just how much defense my new mahogany armor had. It had much more defense than my plain wooden armor! I could continue exploring the jungle without being killed by the powerful enemies. They were much easier to kill since I had more defense, and I could last longer in a fight. I killed a piranha with my enchanted boomerang, and I picked up a hook! I stored it with my supplies and traveled back to the guide so he could explain its use.

It was a long journey back to visit the guide. I found him and said, "While I was exploring the jungle, I picked up a hook from a piranha. What should I do with it?"

"You can craft a grappling hook from the hook dropped from the piranha, but you need to mine some iron to make an anvil and chains," the guide said.

I left the guide and went in search of a cave to look for iron. It wasn't long before I found a cave and had enough iron for what I needed. I took the iron back to my house and crafted an anvil, which I placed on the roof. After finishing the anvil, I had one more iron bar left in my supplies, which allowed me to craft ten chains. Ten chains was more than enough for a grappling hook. I crafted my grappling hook and headed back out to test it. After throwing the grappling hook, the claws grabbed onto a boulder, and it started to pull me in. I tried to stand my ground, but it was just too powerful. I flew through the air and landed on the boulder. Thankfully, I didn't take any damage to my health, and I decided my grappling hook would prove very useful if I found myself in a tough position.

3

Making Houses

After chopping wood for hours, I finally had enough to build five more houses. Floor, roof, wall, table, chair, slime. Wait, what?!! There were four slimes near my build site. It was operation enchanted boomerang time! Oh, yeah! I got three slimes in one strike and focused my attention on the fourth. I groaned when I missed it. After all my practice, I had missed an easy target. Thunk! Second time was the charm. I returned to building.

After I finished the final house, I decided to walk back to the cave where I had mined the iron ore. The walk was pretty boring, but I soon spotted the cave entrance. I was tired of my old copper pickaxe; therefore, I needed to mine enough platinum ore to upgrade it! I had been mining for a bit and stopped to count my ore. I had mined one hundred twenty platinum ore. It was time to walk back home to smelt the ore to make thirty platinum bars. Yay! I used the anvil and my platinum bars to craft a platinum pickaxe. What could I mine with it? CRIMTANE! I had seen a chunk of it in my mine.

The next morning, I returned to the mine, and I mined enough crimtane to craft ten bars. I needed to defeat the Brain of Cthulhu before I could craft crimtane items. I had lots of work to do to be prepared for that fight.

I decided to build more houses and headed out to the forest. It was fun chopping tall trees with my copper axe. I planted saplings to replace them so I didn't lose all of my thick forest. I kept chopping until I had nine hundred ninety-nine pieces of wood. Wow! I had enough wood to build a village! Over the course of two days, I built twenty more houses! I didn't have any words for how excited I was. It was HUGE! I kept building until I completed thirty-five houses. I was at a loss for words!

After my village was finished, I decided to mine some stone. On my way to mine the huge boulder I had spotted in the cave, I killed thirteen slimes. After building all of the houses for the village, I needed to replenish my slime chest since it was running low.

I kept mining stone until I reached my one hundredth block, my five hundredth block, and finally my nine hundred ninety-ninth block! I decided I had enough stone to last me a long time! At that point, I thought I better check in with the guide to ask for more information.

"Hey, what should I do next? I've already crafted a platinum pickaxe."

"You need to build a large flat space for a boss fight arena."

"Okay, thanks! I guess I'll start building. I'll build it one hundred sixty feet long. That should be good enough. I can always come back later and build on."

"You should also grab seeds."

"I'll give it a try. Thanks and see you later."

After I built my arena, I gathered ten of every seed I could find on top of the world. I assumed that would be enough. I built an eight feet tall by twenty feet wide garden shed near my house, and I smelted some sand to make a window so the light could come through. I built separate sections to grow all of the seeds so they wouldn't be contaminated by the deadly crimson seeds. I looked over all I had accomplished that day, and I was happy. I had completed a good day's work and needed to rest!

4

Trading Items

All of the villagers were talking about the Eye of Cthulhu coming so I started my preparations for that battle. I crafted five hundred wooden arrows and a lead bow. I also thought it would be best to upgrade my armor to tungsten so I headed toward the mine.

On my walk to the mine, I didn't see any slimes, which was pretty unusual. I didn't know what had happened to all of them, but I decided to worry about that later. It was time to focus on mining. I mined enough tungsten ore to craft eighty bars, which I thought would be enough for a full suit of armor. I headed back home to get to work on my armor and to get it crafted as soon as possible.

Thankfully, I was correct about the amount of tungsten I needed. I tried on my newly crafted tungsten armor. Yeah! I had higher defense. I left my house to trade in some of my useless items for money, and I also decided to use an extra eight heart crystals. Luckily, I had a chest in one of the other houses in the village just for storing my heart crystals.

I'd just arrived to open the chest when I heard more villagers talking about their nightmares of the Eye of Cthulhu coming. I was beginning to believe the Eye of Cthulhu really was coming. Anyway, I used up all eight heart crystals. Bam! One hundred sixty more health! I had more than enough power to beat the Eye of Cthulhu, and I would get crimtane ore from that battle. Then, I would defeat the Brain of Cthulhu and get some tissue. I was thinking about all of the things I could do, but I decided I better return to the task at hand. I needed to trade and get some money and check in with the guide. I wondered what other preparations I needed to make.

My trading got me twenty-four gold coins, which was enough for what I needed at that point. I found the guide and asked, "How should I prepare for the Eye of Cthulhu boss fight?"

"You need to upgrade your armor to platinum. You also need to make your arena go up into the sky to dodge the Eye of Cthulhu's dash attack."

I left the village and headed to the mine. I needed to mine all of the ore I could get so I could craft platinum armor to exceed the tungsten defense. When I finished in the mine, I had enough platinum ore to craft eighty bars, and then I crafted my new platinum armor. As the guide suggested, I needed to craft wooden platforms every eight blocks up in my arena so I could fight the Eye of Cthulhu in the air. To build all of the wooden platforms, I needed to chop about eight hundred wood from the saplings that I had planted, which would give me one thousand six hundred platforms.

After I chopped the wood, I focused all of my energy on building the platforms. Man, I could have gone up into space! I didn't have enough to reach the top of the world, but I was pretty close! After my platforms were finished, my arena was complete, and all I could think about was how I just needed to get some sleep.

5

Cthulhu Visit

"The Eye of Cthulhu has awoken."

What?! Who said that? What's that roar? AHHHH! A giant eyeball was inside my house! I needed to get out fast! I ran out the door. The oversized eyeball followed me and was rapidly catching up to me. It was time to use my bow. I had not practiced much and was not very good with the bow, but I needed a weapon for long range attacks. Even though I shot my bow as fast as I could, the Eye of Cthulhu just wouldn't die.

The Eye of Cthulhu was catching up to me and soon hit me. I needed to distract it; otherwise, when I waded through the river to the arena, the Eye of Cthulhu would kill me. I needed to build a platform over the water. I had never been in a situation where I had to build so quickly before, but I thought I could do it by placing blocks as fast as I could.

I immediately placed the first block as I reached the river, and I made it halfway across before the big, scary eyeball hit me again. It hurt very badly. I flew up into the air and took some fall damage, but I kept on running. I made it to the arena before the Eye of Cthulhu hit me a third time. I kept climbing up, but I couldn't go up the platforms very quickly. The Eye of Cthulhu was catching up to me again. I started using my enchanted boomerang, and I tossed it as fast as I could. How I wished it would come back faster! The boomerang seemed to be more effective than the bow against the bloody Eye of Cthulhu so the boomerang was the weapon I decided to use most in the fight. I would need a better weapon to kill the Brain of Cthulhu, but I only focused on the battle in front of me.

The Eye of Cthulhu hit me again. I didn't get knocked up into the air, but the hit hurt terribly. If I hadn't been wearing my platinum armor, I would have been dead meat! The Eye of Cthulhu was on half health.

What in the world?! The eye suddenly split into teeth, and it started to roar and dart really quickly at me. It did even more damage. AHHH! I flew really high up into the air. Luckily, I landed on a platform and didn't take fall damage, but I still took twenty damage from the Eye of Cthulhu's hit. I needed to throw the boomerang really quickly. I figured out the Eye of Cthulhu couldn't change direction when darting. That knowledge proved to be very useful. I just needed to use my enchanted boomerang. The Eye of Cthulhu was at quarter health, but I was also at quarter health. After I climbed to the top of the arena, I kept falling down the platforms to dodge the attacks and to avoid being chomped by the Eye of Cthulhu, but it kept darting faster. I was almost to the bottom of the arena, and I needed to boomerang more quickly than ever before. Only twenty more hits left to kill the Eye of Cthulhu! Fifteen! Fourteen! Ten! Five! One! It was dead! Yeah! I picked up the crimtane ore. After that long battle, I headed straight home with my new loot.

6

Making a Mine

When I woke up, I decided it was time to design an easy way to navigate the mine. I would come up with a plan on my walk there. I would need all of my stone to smooth out the mine. The slime rate was normal again because I was seeing more around. I realized the slimes had hidden when the Eye of Cthulhu came. I didn't blame them. That was one powerful, destructive eyeball! First, I made the mine floor smooth. Then, it was time to even out the walls and roof of the mine.

As I placed the last block on the floor, I encountered a new slime. It was a red slime, and it was coming toward me to attack. I charged at it and got two hits in before it dashed at me. I jumped and struck the red slime again with my sword to kill it. That red slime was the most powerful slime I had encountered to date!

I finished the roof and found an underground lake

with green luminescent jellyfish while exploring. I mined all of the rare minerals along the way. After I had smoothed out the walls, I decided to mine more ore.

After I finished my mining, I counted two full stacks of stone and four hundred platinum ore. I had six hundred tungsten ore, nine hundred ninety copper ore, and eight hundred iron ore. I hoped I had enough to build a larger arena to fight bosses.

My greatest discovery during my day of mining was finding a magic mirror in a chest inside the mine. The mirror could be used to teleport back to my home, but it would give me side effects like nausea. I decided not to use it except under extreme cases. I just left the mine like normal and walked to the arena to expand its size. I planned to build the arena one hundred feet longer. I also planned to chop more trees to get enough platforms to expand the new part into the sky.

Oh, there was the guide up ahead. I wanted to talk to him. "What do I need to do to prepare for upcoming boss encounters?"

"Look out because King Slime very rarely spawns on the outer two-thirds of the world. If you build a tall rope, he can't teleport up to you."

"I'm going to pack up to head to the ocean on the far edge of the world anyway. I don't think I need to worry about King Slime if it's so rare for it to spawn."

"Be careful if there is a dungeon. If you talk to the old man, Skeletron will spawn. You should also go exploring into the sky to look for a sky island. They offer excellent loot, but beware of the flying harpies. They can easily kill you."

Before I left the village, I met with the merchant and spent about four gold on supplies for my journey to the ocean. As I walked, I hunted for more slimes to have a good supply of gel on hand. I killed forty-one slimes and decided that would be enough. I was excited to be headed off to the ocean to explore more of the world, and I wondered what new things I would see.

7

Exploring the World

I planned to return with the new items from my adventure to the ocean within four weeks. I wasn't worried about King Slime since the guide said the chances of it spawning were very low. I had walked for a day when I came upon the crimson cave. I discovered I didn't like the chimeras from the crimson cave because they could fly, and I didn't have a weapon to fight them because my boomerang wasn't fast enough. My platinum sword only did fifteen damage. I needed a better sword.

I finally made it to the dungeon, and I remembered the guide's warning about Skeletron spawning if I talked to the old man. I grabbed the dungeon bed at the dungeon entrance, but instead of entering the dungeon, I built a bridge over it. I couldn't afford to get killed by Skeletron. I looked back at the dungeon and just kept walking until I finally reached the ocean. With all of my adventures during my walk, it took me a week and a half to reach the ocean! As soon as I arrived, I built a house so I could get some much needed rest.

It was morning. What woke me up? A blue slime! Thunk! Taking care of the blue slime was easy. Hmm, my travel here took much longer than I expected. I discovered that there wasn't a jungle on that side of the world, which was good to know.

It was time to build a fort with my wood and stone, but I needed to pick out a spot to fish first. I located a good spot and built a fishing dock, and then I built a couple of platforms. When I started on the fort, I decided to build the right side first because that was where the goblin scouts would invade since they couldn't enter from the ocean side. I built the wall three blocks thick so if I accidentally used a bomb while mining, the wall would stop the explosion. Then, I built the wall on the left side of the fort. I built a guardrail on the end of the fishing dock so I couldn't fall into the ocean. I was not planning on adding a roof. What could go wrong? I flattened the ground to make it easy to walk across. When my fort was finished, I started thinking about a name. I knew right away! Fort Terra! The name fit.

After I named the fort, I turned my attention to building an emergency room. The emergency room walls were five blocks thick and partially underground. The emergency room was located at the corner of my fort so the fort walls also added thickness to two walls of the emergency room. The emergency room had torches, a furnace, a crafting bench, an anvil, and three chests. Everything I needed! After I finished the fort's emergency room, I went out to go fishing before I took a break to rest.

"King Slime has awoken."

Who said that? Wait, KING SLIME?! I needed to get inside the fort's emergency room immediately!

8

King Slime Time

As I stood inside the fort's emergency room, I wondered how I was going to kill King Slime. If I opened the emergency room door I would be suffocated by the slimes. There were blue slimes, not green, waiting for me outside the door. That was even worse! I had to think! I tried to remember what the guide said about King Slime. He said if I built a rope that went high in the air, King Slime couldn't get me. I decided to open the emergency room door and make a run for it! Right away, I was suffocated by all of the slimes, and it was hard to breathe. I ran for the tower staircase on the right side of the fort. I ran as fast as I could, but the slimes were being shot up the stairs. I could see the top of the tower. I was nearly there. I was using my enchanted boomerang, but it wasn't working because there were just too many slimes. If I was going to survive, I needed a better plan. It was my time to shine!

When I was in the village to pick up supplies for the trip to the ocean, I had bought some bombs from the demolitionist. That was it! I started throwing bombs super fast. Ahhh! I was blown into the air by the explosions, but I used my grappling hook to reach safety. I was knocked unconscious as debris from the blast flew around me and crashed into my head.

When I finally woke up, it was morning and everything was peaceful. I tried to move, but I couldn't. I yelled for help, but none came. I noticed a slimy saddle had been added to my supplies. I summoned it and used all of my strength to get on the friendly slime and pointed it in the direction of the village. That was the last thing I remember.

I woke up in the village with the nurse sewing my leg. I tried to get up, but something was wrong. "My right arm! It's broken!"

"Yeah, that broken arm should teach you a lesson not to use hundreds of explosives to kill King Slime," the nurse said.

"Okay, but how will I survive with only one useable arm?"

"I have a sling you can use. It is not very good, but it will do. You'll have to use the slime mount to get around for the next month," the nurse said.

"Okay, but how will I use a sword if I don't have

an arm to balance with?"

"You will need a summon weapon to protect yourself."

"I have a slime staff! It makes me so happy that I lucked up and got one," I said.

"Good, and you can use a gun. Also you can set your arm so you can hold a bow. Your surgery will cost four gold."

"Okay," I said as I tried to get up. As I sat up, I noticed my right leg looked like a chew toy. "Ahhhh!" and I fainted.

9

Preparation

The nurse said I would need to be on the slime mount for a month, and my right side would be more prone to injuries because of my arm. How could things get worse? I loved having the slime staff since I couldn't protect myself. Not long after my surgery, I went in the evil biome, the crimson, to collect heart crystals. I wasn't able to fight so I only broke two crimson hearts and decided to wait until I was feeling better to break the third, which would summon the Brain of Cthulhu. I waited for the meteorites to land since I had broken the crimson hearts. After they landed, I could mine them. I kept getting hurt by the crimson enemies like the face monster chimera. I should have built an arena.

I left the crimson to return to inspect Fort Terra to determine how much damage the bombs caused. I could only move a bit faster than walking since I was using the slime mount, but I finally made it. WOW! The fort dropped off, and I couldn't see the other side. It was time to start the repairs!

After the repairs were complete, Fort Terra looked just like before. I built a staircase to the hole the bombs created. It went all the way down to the bottom of the world. Since I didn't have other work to do at Fort Terra, I decided to return to the village to visit a sky island like the guide suggested.

When I arrived back in the village, I climbed up to the sky island using my rope ladder. I picked up a horseshoe and a star fury. The star fury was my new favorite weapon! I trained myself to use it single-handed. The star fury shot a star down from the sky! As a few harpies flew around me, I decided to test my new weapon. The star fury killed the harpies in one or two hits. I examined the horseshoe. Negates fall damage?! I needed to test it, too! I took one step off sky island...

"Is a meteorite falling on my house? Wait, it's Eric! NOOO! I will have to sew him up again!" the nurse yelled.

"Wow, it worked! The horseshoe really worked!" Why did the nurse faint? "Nurse, what's wrong? Wake up!" I approached the nurse, but a harpy flew down and headed straight for me. It launched some feathers and crack! My leg broke again. Oof!

"How do you sleep through a surgery? It's free

since I fainted on you earlier," the nurse said as I woke up.

"What's your name?" I asked.

"Kelly."

"Am I free to go now?"

"Yes, but be careful. I upgraded the sling to a bendable cast so you can use a sword."

"Thanks! Bye, Nurse Kelly."

"Bye, Eric!"

Five weeks had passed since the discovery of the star fury and my surgery, and I no longer felt pain when moving around. It was still difficult to walk but not impossible. I had traveled back to check in on things at Fort Terra. There was still bomb debris everywhere, but the fort was in good shape. Other than a quick check, I didn't plan to spend any more time at the fort so I returned to the village.

10

Meteor Mash

I went in search of the merchant when I returned to the village. I walked in the merchant's house, and it started rumbling. I had no idea what was going on. I looked out the window, and a meteor was headed straight for me! I tried to run out of the house and reach safety, but the door had jammed. I threw all of my extra bombs at the door, but it was too late. Bam! The meteor hit the merchant's house, and the roof started to cave in. The last thing I remember was a chunk of meteorite hitting my chest.

"HOW DO YOU SURVIVE WITH YOUR STUPID IDEAS?!" Nurse Kelly yelled.

"Where am I?"

"The emergency room that you built in the village's underground bunker. The rest of the village was blown sky high. Now, you are one big scar. You've been unconscious for days. The merchant rebuilt the village for you," Nurse Kelly said.

"Okay, bye. I need to go. I have things I need to do."

"Bye? That's all you have to say? I don't know how you do it. How can you be so reckless?" Nurse Kelly said as she shook her head.

"That's pretty much all I have to say. I've already wasted too much time. I need to head back to Fort Terra on my slime mount," I said as I left the bunker. The nurse just stared at me like I was crazy.

I arrived back at Fort Terra, and I crafted full meteor armor and a space gun from the meteor that hit the village. I also had full mana to give me magic power and a star cannon with eight hundred ammo. I was finally ready to fight the Brain of Cthulhu, who lived in the crimson. It would take me about a week to travel to there!

After I arrived at the crimson cave entrance, I built a small shelter to stay in until it was time to fight the Brain of Cthulhu. I had all of my weapons ready, but I was waiting for the rain to stop. I didn't need the rain bringing out any more powerful enemies that I would have to fight. It finally stopped raining, and I entered the crimson cave to start building the arena for the battle with the Brain of Cthulhu. I built one story of the arena at a time until I had completed all four stories.

It had been four days since I finished building the arena. Bam! Another meteor! It traveled down the cave tunnel and landed in the middle of the arena. I mined it quickly. I had crafted an obsidian skull to protect me from fire damage so the meteorite didn't burn me. I mined enough meteorite ore to craft eighty meteorite bars, which I thought should be enough to last. I was ready for my fight with the Brain of Cthulhu! I broke my third and last crimson heart, and I started running through the arena. I hoped that I would win because I knew it would be a tough battle.

11

Brain Game

"The Brain of Cthulhu has awoken."

I focused only on killing the Brain of Cthulhu at first, but I couldn't kill it. I finally decided I needed to kill the servants first. They dropped tissue and ore. I also needed some crowd control. Sticky grenades. Boom! All of the servants dropped dead. Star cannon time. Wow, the Brain of Cthulhu hadn't even touched me. After the Brain of Cthulhu reached half health, he teleported and hit me! That was cheap! How would I kill it? I knew! I unleashed the slime staff, which summoned a baby slime to fight for me! The baby slime joined me in attacking the Brain of Cthulhu. The slime was destroying the Brain of Cthulhu, and I continued firing my star cannon. The Brain of Cthulhu hit me, and I flew into the air. I needed twenty more hits. I kept firing my star cannon. Ten. Five. Two. One. Zero. I killed it! I killed the Brain of Cthulhu! I finally had everything I needed to craft crimtane armor! With crimtane armor, I could defeat the Queen Bee with ease. I had a list of items I needed to craft before that battle: the artery yo-yo, crimtane armor, meatball, tendon bow, the pickaxe and the blood butcherer. I had to travel to Fort Terra to start crafting!

I arrived back at Fort Terra, and I crafted everything I needed. With my new items, I would be ready to fight Skeletron after I defeated the Queen Bee, and with a bit of arena building, I would have the supplies I needed to progress to the Wall of Flesh. It was time to find the bee hive!

I arrived at the jungle, and the enemies were easy to defeat with the artery yo-yo. I saw spiked jungle slimes. Ow! They shot spikes! I pulled out the tendon bow and finished them off. I kept moving through the jungle, and I finally saw the beehive. It was small and yellow and dripping with honey. I tried to get in, but bees were shot out at me when I hit a block. Ahh! I tried digging faster, but the bees kept coming. I finally reached the inside, and I saw the larva in the middle. I set up the arena because I wanted to be prepared before I tried to fight the Queen Bee. I had platforms every five blocks up to make sure I could defeat the Queen Bee easily. I left the hive and set up a base just outside so I could collect ore and more tools.

I was finally ready to fight the Queen Bee. I went back inside the hive and walked toward the larva. Whack!

12

Bee Business

"The Queen Bee has awoken."

Star cannon time! I only had two stars because I had left the rest in a chest back in the village! I couldn't use a star fury because I was underground. What would I do? I needed to use the tendon bow, but I didn't have any arrows. Blood butcherer? No, I needed a long-range weapon! Artery yo-yo, then. Bam! The Queen Bee surely felt that first strike! The artery yo-yo worked really well. Oww. The Queen Bee shot stingers at me! Uhhh, what was I doing? Ahhh, confused debuff from the Queen Bee's stingers! The artery yo-yo dealt more damage until the Queen Bee was at half health and started darting at me. I received the poison debuff from the Queen Bee's stingers, and I needed to heal. Gulp! I drank a healing potion and felt much better right away! I could think clearly again.

SPACE GUN! Where was it? I found it, and bam! The space gun was working! The Queen Bee was at quarter health, but I needed to do a little more damage. Ahhh! The Queen Bee hit me, and I flew into the air. I stopped firing. My mana was out, and I didn't have any mana potions! For my mana to recharge, I needed to stay still, but I couldn't do that without turning into a squashed bug! The artery yo-yo still worked, but it wasn't fast enough. I couldn't even use grenades without getting hit! How would I win? Bang! I got stabbed by stingers. I kept using my artery yo-yo, but I couldn't kill the Queen Bee. I had a great idea! I could fire three grenades then fall down the platforms to dodge the explosion, and the Queen Bee would ram into the grenades as she darted at me.

Boom! The Queen Bee darted toward me but hit my three grenades instead. I only had five grenades left, and I needed exactly five to kill her. I made four direct hits, which dropped the Queen Bee to sixty health. Last grenade! Bang! It only did fifty damage so I pulled out the artery yo-yo again. The Queen Bee hit me, and I fell down into the honey. I couldn't get out, but I remembered my grappling hook and used it to pull myself free. I continued using my artery yo-yo and managed to kill the Queen Bee. I did it! I looked through my supplies and saw honeyed goggles and a bee gun. I summoned the bee mount and flew toward the entrance of the hive. When I left the hive,

I built a house in the jungle to survive the night and immediately fell asleep.

13

Skeletron Time

I left the jungle on my bee mount and headed toward the dungeon. Halfway there, I stopped by the village to craft a hornet staff and to collect arrows and supplies so I would be prepared to fight Skeletron. After I left the village, I stopped in the middle of the snow biome for a rest to save my bee mount's energy because it gave me more mobility for the battle. I switched to my slime mount when I decided to leave the snow biome. It took me three weeks from the time I left the jungle to reach the dungeon. I filled the entrance to the dungeon with dirt to eliminate the risk of me falling into the dungeon and the dungeon guardian spawning and destroying everything. During the day, I built another arena on top of the dungeon to ensure a successful battle with Skeletron, and I continued to prepare for the upcoming battle by brewing potions. I planned to use my star cannon to make it an easy win. It started turning right, and I walked over to the old man near the dungeon.

"I beg you to free me of my curse," said the old man.

"Okay…"

"Skeletron has awoken."

I immediately shot four stars at Skeletron, but every single one missed. I needed to use the star fury. Bam! Direct hit. Ahh! Skeletron's left hand slapped me in the face, and I got smashed into a dungeon pillar. I used the bee gun, and killer bees swarmed Skeletron. I looked at Skeletron's health, and its head was down only one quarter. I aimed with the star cannon again and fired eight stars. Four stars hit each of Skeletron's hands, which destroyed both hands. I pulled out the tendon bow, and I fired fifteen arrows, and six arrows hit Skeletron's head. After that, he was less than one quarter health. I used the star fury to make a star land on Skeletron's head. Skeletron disappeared and left behind the book of skulls and Skeletron's hand.

After the battle, I couldn't move my neck so I hopped on the bee mount and flew to the ocean to recover at Fort Terra. I still wasn't using the magic mirror to travel because teleporting was dangerous. It made me puke and increased the risk of me splitting in two. The risk was way too high for me!

After recovering, I left Fort Terra and traveled back to the village. I replenished my supplies and health before I started getting ready to fight the Wall of Flesh.

"A goblin army is approaching from the east."

What?! I knew exactly what to do.

"Everyone in the village must prepare for war with the goblins! We will fight to keep our rights!"

14

Goblin Party

"A goblin army has arrived."

"Fire at will!" I shouted.

Boom! Every goblin who got close to the village walls was disintegrated. Ahh! The goblins started throwing spiky balls, which injured many villagers. Nurse Kelly couldn't keep up with all of the injuries and heal everyone. Seeing the destruction, I realized what we needed. Killer bees! All of the goblins near me were killed by a huge swarm of killer bees from my bee gun. The demolitionist was throwing bombs. Everyone wanted the goblins gone.

After a magic goblin shot a magic ball out and made the villagers fly into the air, the villagers all ran and hid. I used the star cannon to hit the magic goblin, but the magic goblin shot another magic ball. It made me fall to the ground, but then I ran up and used the star fury on the goblin. The magic goblin couldn't hit me, and I got in one final hit and killed it. I looked around to discover that we had cleared out the goblins. Even though most of the villagers were injured, they started cheering. We had a lot of upgrading to perform on the village defenses after the goblin attack.

I was helping the villagers pick up the spiky balls when I heard shouting.

"There are goblins in the west sector!" a man yelled.

All of the villagers who were still able to fight ran to the west side. A bunch of goblins were trying to kill a block of wood. Everyone stared.

"Umm, okay...," the merchant said.

The demolitionist threw a grenade. Thunk!

"Okay, problem solved," I said. "We need to check the towers. Oww! It's raining spiky balls. Get in the armor room!"

There were at least twenty goblins on the roof throwing spiky balls down at us. Everyone started running up the stairs.

"Stop!" I yelled, but it was too late. Hundreds of spiky balls came rolling down the stairs, and all of the villagers turned and ran out the door. I blocked the door with dirt, but twenty spiky balls escaped and hit the villagers, severely injuring them. I used my hornet staff ,and the hornets went to the roof, which made the goblins start jumping off the tower. The villagers killed the goblins as they landed. I used the artery yo-yo to finish the job. All of the remaining goblins huddled in a corner. I took out the star fury, and I used a star to hit them all at once.

All of the goblins' coins flew into the air, and the coins just kept bouncing. I collected forty-three gold! The villagers resumed their trading like nothing had happened. All was well.

15

Super Upgrade

After the goblins were defeated, I decided it was time to fight the Wall of Flesh. I used a bone rattle from my battle with the Brain of Cthulhu to summon a baby face monster. I needed all the help I could get. I left the village to travel to Fort Terra, and I stopped at the dungeon to grab a water candle. When I left the dungeon, I summoned my bee mount and the hornet staff. I reached Fort Terra, and I went down the stairs to the underworld. I built a hut to craft in. I filled one hundred lava buckets to start building an obsidian mine, but I needed more ore. I mined around twenty bars worth of the special underworld ore, and I used a forge I found in the underworld to smelt it. A mine cart track helped me to collect ore more efficiently. When I had enough ore, I started building the obsidian mine.

I built a medium sized obsidian mine with a water

pool. As the lava leaked into the water pool, I could make eight obsidian blocks at a time. I had a little extra obsidian left over to store with my supplies in the case of an emergency. I crafted everything I needed for the battle against the Wall of Flesh, but I still needed to build a flat floor two thousand blocks long. I made the floor out of stone since I had four stacks of it, and I had a few dart traps that would help with the fight against the Wall of Flesh. I still needed to farm for the underworld yo-yo and the magic book. The guide did not give me any tips about defeating the Wall of Flesh. I wondered why.

I stayed down in the underworld after the floor was completed. I had a water candle and dart traps to auto farm, and I had crafted an imp staff, which protected me against enemies. I had all of the tools I needed except the magic book. I was struggling to kill all of the enemies spawned by the water candle. Thwack! I killed an enemy and finally got the magic book! It shot out a scythe, which was super powerful! Boom! The magic book killed a bone serpent, and the yo-yo that it dropped was called cascade. I needed a few more upgrades from the goblin tinkerer, and then I would be ready to fight the Wall of Flesh!

I arrived at the village to visit the goblin tinkerer and received all of the reforged items I needed. I bought purification powder because I thought I would need it. When it was time to fight, I flew on the bee mount to the edge of the world, and I threw the guide voodoo doll, which dropped from an enemy in the underworld, into the lava. I wondered what it did to the guide.

Meanwhile, the guide limped into Nurse Kelly's office.

"What happened Andrew? There are burn marks all over you," Nurse Kelly said.

The guide burst into flames.

"What has Eric done now?!"

"The Wall of Flesh has awoken."

16

Flesh Fight

"The guide was slain."

What did I just do? I decided the guide would not die in vain! The hungry were chomping at my arm, and I used my bee gun to destroy them. The Wall of Flesh shot lasers at me, and I flew into a building and was jammed into a block. The Wall of Flesh moved toward me. As it passed, it grabbed me and flung me one hundred blocks away, and I crunched against the wall. I remembered I had dynamite sitting in my supplies. I knew if I was going to survive I needed to kill the Wall of Flesh quickly. I was about to throw the dynamite when the Wall of Flesh grabbed me and flung me again. All of the dynamite flew out of my grasp, and I hit a house and broke my arm. My head slammed against the wall, and it made my thinking fuzzy.

I tried to use the flamerang I had crafted, but my

aiming was off. My pet baby face monster was mad! When the Wall of Flesh shot another laser, it made my baby face monster scream, and the Wall of Flesh blew up. I temporarily went deaf, but I quickly gathered all of the loot from the Wall of Flesh. I got a clockwork assault rifle, a breaker blade and a pwnhammer.

I headed back to the village. My brain was still confused because of the hit I took, but I finally managed to make it to the nurse. Nurse Kelly took one look at me and sighed.

"What is it with you and bombs? If I didn't know any better, the demolitionist has possessed you. You've had as many 'incidents' as him."

"How much do I have to pay you this time?"

"Only two gold. You get a discount for coming here so many times."

"Here you go." I handed the money over to the frustrated nurse.

"Goodbye, and don't come back," Nurse Kelly said as I started toward the door.

"I don't plan on it." Did she really think I enjoyed all of these injuries?

"Wait, aren't you sorry you killed the guide?"

"Oh, he doesn't respawn?"

"He does, but aren't you even a little sad?" asked Nurse Kelly.

I was really sad the guide had to die. I really liked all of the villagers. I didn't want any of them to die even if they did respawn. "Well the past is the past, though I do really like the guide." Wait a minute. "Do I respawn?"

"No, you would never see daylight again."

17

Super Smasher Bros

A week later, I bumped into the guide in the village. Thankfully, the guide looked fully healed and back to normal, but boy, did he look mad at me.

"Hello, Eric…," the guide said in an accusing tone.

"Sorry! I'm so sorry that I killed you fighting the Wall of Flesh. I didn't know what would happen."

"It's okay. You had to do it, but don't try that again," the guide said.

"So now that I've killed the Wall of Flesh and unlocked hardmode, what should I do?" I asked.

"Even though you killed me, I'll still give you some tips. Go break the alters in the crimson to unlock the new hardmode ores, but beware of the new stronger enemies."

Before I left for the crimson, I climbed to the top of my arena near the village to find a wyvern, a dragon that lived and flew high in the sky. A few hours passed before I spotted a white wyvern and used my clockwork assault rifle. It dropped souls of flight that I could craft into a pair of wings. I immediately left the arena and flew on my bee mount to the snow biome. I had not been there since before my fight with Skeletron. I farmed the amarok yo-yo, which was easy to find since it was a one in three hundred drop chance. The amarok yo-yo was one of the top three weapons in my supplies. It was so powerful it could slay any enemy with ease.

Later that day, I flew the bee mount to the left crimson cave to break the alters. Whoa! As soon as I entered the crimson, a herpling flung me into the air, but I used my new wings to steady myself. I used the cascade yo-yo from the bone serpent, which easily chopped through all of the enemies I encountered. I picked up a soul of night from a crimson enemy, and I also got a blade tongue from fishing in the crimson. They were useful in destroying all of the crimson enemies, which took me a long time.

My goal was to destroy all of the alters so I could start operation mining mayhem. I destroyed my first alter and then destroyed one after another. Boom! I got palladium. Bang! I got mythril. Bang! I got titanium. Oh no! Fifty wraiths appeared. Clank! I took out a few with the blade tongue, and the amarok yo-yo ripped apart the rest. It was time to break the next alters. As I broke the next set of alters, I picked up the hardmode ores, and I had to fight the wraiths again.

I needed a magic weapon to destroy enemies so I blew a cavern in the underground crimson. I was hopeful to get a magic dagger by killing a mimic. Right away, three mimics cornered me against a wall! I tried to kill them with the blade tongue, but they were too powerful. I boxed myself in stone, and I created a one block gap to use the amarok yo-yo, which destroyed them in seconds! The amarok yo-yo saved my life! I got a grappling hook, a magic dagger, and a daedalus stormbow! I thought the items I picked up would do quite well.

I left the crimson underground and returned to the village to find the goblin tinkerer, and he reforged my new items to increase their damage. I spent forty gold at the goblin tinkerer's shop. Then, I decided to travel to my mine, which was a four hour flight on the bee mount, to mine some hardmode ore. I was puzzled by why the blue slimes were trying to jump and reach me, but I just kept flying.

18

Mining Mayhem

It was time for operation mining mayhem! First, I planned to mine the palladium ore, which was easy to find. After I mined my tenth block off the mine floor, I used my grappling hook to collect the palladium ore in the ceiling of the caverns. I spotted some glowing mushroom grass seed to make a mini surface biome, but I decided to stay focused on mining until I had enough palladium ore. I mined two hundred palladium ore so I could craft the armor and the drill. I thought about mining enough palladium ore for the sword, but I decided I didn't need the sword since the breaker blade did more damage. After I finished mining palladium ore, I returned to the village to craft my palladium items before I returned to the mine. When I was crafting, the guide stopped by my house.

"Hi, I just came back from mining palladium," I said. "Do you have any tips for me going forward?"

"Look for a drax inside a shadow chest in the underworld. It will mine almost anything," the guide said. "The key you found in the dungeon chest will open shadow chests."

"Thanks for the tips. I'll check it out!"

I left the village and flew to the mine. It was time to mine the mythril ore! First, I mined the huge chunk of mythril I found in the bottom of the mine. Wait! I couldn't forget my talk with the guide about a drax in a shadow chest. I had the dungeon key in my supplies, so I just needed to start opening shadow chests to find the drax. I remembered there was a shadow chest at the bottom of the staircase to the underworld at Fort Terra, and I could get to it easily.

After I arrived at Fort Terra, I immediately went down the stairs to the shadow chest. I hoped that the drax would be in that one because I didn't want to search all around the underworld. I opened the chest, and I got the drax, which had two hundred pickaxe power! I could mine everything I needed. I focused on mining the mythril ore before I could mine titanium and upgrade my armor, which I needed to do to ensure victory against the Destroyer. I saw a chunk of mythril in the bottom of the hole and went to work until I had enough mythril ore for armor. I was ready to move on to titanium mining, but I first needed to craft my mythril items. Luckily, I had an anvil at the top of Fort Terra, and I started to climb up the stairs. It was a long climb since the hole went all the way down to the bottom of the world. I finally arrived at the top and crafted my mythril armor.

I remembered a huge cavern that was right above the underworld where I knew I would find some titanium. It was only about an hour away from Fort Terra. When I reached the cavern, I plugged the holes to make sure I was alone. I had the drax, so I didn't need titanium ore for the drill. I mined just enough titanium ore to craft the armor and sword. I had upgraded my furnace to a titanium forge; therefore, I was able to craft the ore into titanium bars. Then, I crafted the titanium armor and sword. The armor made a weird blur effect. I had forty-nine defense plus my accessories, which gave me a grand total of fifty-four defense!

19

A Chill Creeps Down My Spine

I returned to the arena near the village, and I placed heart lanterns everywhere to boost regeneration of my health. I felt a tremor beneath the earth and decided I was ready for the battle.

"The Destroyer has awoken."

I had prepared for that moment, and I hoped all of my preparations would help me to succeed. Wow! The Destroyer was a giant mechanical worm. Whoa! Its minions shot lasers, and I needed a crowd control weapon. I thought the meteor staff would be helpful because I needed to be long range for the fight, and I needed to stay focused.

The Destroyer had high health so I had to rely on mana. Speaking of mana, mine was drained! I was so distracted that I hadn't noticed it had run out. I needed a yo-yo, and the amarok was the best I had. I was very glad I had a snow biome. It was small, but it got the job done for farming weapons. Oh! The amarok yo-yo was useless against the Destroyer because it didn't pierce multiple segments. I was in a tough position. I had been through a lot, but the battle with the Destroyer was the most difficult by far.

Ahh! The Destroyer hit me. It felt like knives were stabbing into me. I got knocked back into wood, which surrounded me so I couldn't move. Fortunately, I had a powerful drax to mine the wood. I had considered storing the drax in my main chest at Fort Terra. Whew, I was glad I hadn't left my drax behind! It felt like I was being ground to shreds. Actually, I was. I could still move around, but it was difficult.

Would the daedalus stormbow work? With the holy arrows, it should defeat the Destroyer! I decided to try. Wow! It tore the Destroyer apart. The daedalus stormbow and holy arrow combination was really good to use on enemies with long bodies and was much more useful than I thought. The holy arrows were defeating the Destroyer because they sent a star falling from the sky when they hit an enemy. I kept shooting the Destroyer, and it should have only taken a minute to kill it using the daedalus stormbow. The battle was easy because all I had to do was fire and wait. As long as I moved to keep from being trapped when the Destroyer tunneled in the earth, I was safe. Oh no! The Destroyer surrounded me and was suffocating me like a boa constrictor! Ow! I got brutally launched into the air out of the Destroyer's grip. As I flew through the air, I turned and fired the daedalus stormbow one last time. The Destroyer dropped to one hundred health, and then the next second, it was dead!

I picked up the loot and returned to the village to craft all of my new items. I crafted the excalibur, hallowed armor, and the light disk.

"Skeletron Prime has awoken."

What?!

20

Mech Battle

A giant skull flew around me, seemingly sizing me up. I was ready for the battle because the daedalus stormbow could take out all four hands at once. Taking out the head would require the newly crafted light discs. Wow, I thought it was easy. I just needed to dodge the hands, and I would be okay. I thought I could most likely kill Skeletron Prime in my sleep. Whoa! Skeletron Prime hit me with its cannon, which really hurt. I couldn't afford to get distracted; otherwise, I would become truffle worm mush. I had taken a third of Skeletron Prime's health already, and if my progress kept up, I was guaranteed to get a good night's rest. Wow! Skeletron Prime was surrounded in spikes and was rolling toward me. Oww! I got shredded and thrown into the air. I hit the ground on my side. I must have broken my arm because I couldn't move it. I thought it was broken at the elbow, but it could be fixed. I needed to pay attention to the battle. I was getting destroyed. I got hit again! Skeletron Prime's saw smashed my arm. If my arm wasn't broken before, it was definitely broken after that hit. I was really glad I had two arms. My imp wasn't helping much, as the armor on Skeletron Prime was crazy! My bee mount was absolutely amazing because I couldn't have dodged Skeletron Prime's attacks on my own. I barely got hit by debris! Skeletron Prime was at half health.

My arm hurt, and I wondered how much I would have to spend to fix it. I thought ten gold would probably cover it. Most of the time I had to use all of the coins that the bosses dropped to cover my medical bills. I really needed a way to remain uninjured while fighting bosses. I would have been shredded by Skeletron Prime without hallowed armor. The titanium was only one less defense, but every little detail made a big difference in a tough battle. I wondered what I could make from Skeletron Prime's awesome loot. I couldn't wait to see, but I needed to kill it first to find out. I thought about leading Skeletron Prime into the village to ask the guide. It wouldn't be too difficult.

As I reached the village, I heard screaming. I wondered why. Knives were being thrown out windows. All of the villagers were attacking the destructive Skeletron Prime. Skeletron Prime was scraping along the walls of the village as he followed me. I came up to the guide's door, and he peeked out as he cracked the door open.

"What do you want, and why is Skeletron Prime knocking down buildings? Everyone thinks we're about to die!"

"I want to know what weapons I can craft from Skeletron Prime's drops."

"A flamethrower. Now get out!" I was abruptly cut off and pushed back from the door as the guide slammed it in my face.

A few minutes later, I made it back to the arena with Skeletron Prime close behind me. I made a few more powerful hits before Skeletron Prime died. I picked up souls of fright, hallowed bars, greater healing potions and coins.

Everyone in the village was angry with me, but I needed Nurse Kelly to treat my wounds.

"Eric, what did you do? Why were you crazy enough to bring Skeletron Prime into the village?" Nurse Kelly yelled as she started working on my arm.

"I'm sorry about that. I was just very curious about what I could craft from Skeletron Prime's drops."

"It's okay. I forgive you. Now, get out of here before I change my mind."

"The Twins have awoken."

21

Double Eyes

Oh, no! I didn't know if I could kill the infamous Twins. Actually, I decided it might be easy with the daedalus stormbow. I hoped so. If I defeated the Twins, I would have killed three bosses in one night. The chances were super rare for a natural spawn of the three mechanical bosses. I didn't know how it happened! Oh wow! The Twins were very aggressive and shot a toxic green substance and lasers. Luckily, the daedalus stormbow damaged both twins at once. Since they each didn't have much health, I could simultaneously kill both with the wide spread damage of the legendary daedalus stormbow, which had saved my life already twice that night. If all went according to plan, everything would work out, but my plans never seemed to work exactly the way I expected.

There had to be more to the Twins, as they were nearing half health, and the battle hadn't been extremely challenging. The Twins started spinning, and their flesh fell off. Then they were plated in hard iron. I discovered that was why they were called a mechanical boss. Whoa! The Twins flew around me at insane speeds and slammed into me. One shot out a line of the toxic green substance, while the other was firing deadly bullets in all directions. Bullet holes were everywhere, and some bullets went as far as the village. The Twins were at roughly one third health. At that point, I didn't know if I would survive the strenuous fight. The Twins kept running around me and throwing debris everywhere. The toxic green substance hit my legs, which immediately deformed, and I fell to the ground. I needed help so I used a flare to let the villagers know I was in deep trouble. I hoped the villagers saw my signal because I only had five flares left and couldn't afford to waste another one.

Arrows started flying toward me because the villagers thought I was the boss! I crawled into a cave near the arena as arrows hit the top of the cave's entrance. The villagers' arrows distracted the Twins so I continued using the daedalus stormbow. The Twins were barely alive. They turned around and around because they didn't know who or what to hit. They fell dead as a bullet from the arms dealer hit each one in the center of their bodies.

I thought the villagers had finally figured out who was the real enemy, but as I crawled out of the cave, arrows, knives and bullets hit me in the chest. I fell to the ground unconscious.

22

Chlorophyte

It took a few months after the brutal fight with the Twins before I had fully recovered. While I was recovering, I found the guide to ask for tips.

"I defeated the Twins. What do I need to do next?"

"You need to go into the jungle to find chlorophyte ore and golden hearts to boost your health," the guide said. "Be careful. The jungle has been upgraded with more difficult enemies. There will also be a Plantera bulb in the jungle, which you can use to summon Plantera when you're ready. Plantera is difficult to defeat but not the most difficult boss."

I left the village and went in search of the ore in the jungle called chlorophyte. It was supposedly one of the strongest ores around. It could be crafted into an armor better then any armor I had so far. I didn't know how difficult the new jungle enemies were so I decided to be very cautious. I had a pirate staff, which was a great minion upgrade from my imp staff. It did so much more damage, and I could tear things up with it.

I entered the jungle, and I spotted a bouncy over-sized beetle jumping around the jungle floor. Wow! A giant turtle hit me in the chest, and I flew through the air. I hit the wet ground and looked at my health. Quarter health! I needed to get the golden hearts the guide told me about. They were supposed to raise my health. My light disk tore through the turtle. It seemed the jungle enemies dealt high damage but had low defense. I entered the nearest cave to mine the chlorophyte, and I set up camp because I thought I would be there a very long time.

A few months passed, and I finally had enough chlorophyte to craft the armor and the claymore. The chlorophyte claymore would do roughly seventy-five damage without accessories or armor. I also had full health with golden hearts. I headed back to the village to craft the supplies to prepare for the fight with the mysterious and super powerful boss, Plantera.

Heading back to the village was more challenging than before the fight with the Wall of Flesh. Defeating the Wall of Flesh and unlocking hardmode changed the world by adding more difficult enemies and a new biome called the hallow. I could see the crimson was spreading fast. I needed to figure out how to stop it so I planned to ask the guide.

I arrived at the village and immediately searched for the guide.

"I've noticed the crimson has been spreading."

"Yes it has," the guide said. "If you want to stop it, you need to buy a clentaminator and some green solution."

I left the guide and went straight to the steampunker to buy a clentaminator with some green solution to clean up the crimson. I also crafted turtle armor from chlorophyte bars and turtle shells, which gave me seventy defense. That was even more than regular chlorophyte! I was deep into my plans to prepare for the battle with Plantera and ran into the guide again.

"Hello. If you don't have much to do, I know how you can get inside the jungle temple easily," the guide said.

"I have a lot of free time right now. If you have any suggestions, I can do them."

"If you hammer on any platform in front of the jungle temple door, you can pass through it without needing a key. You can collect super dart traps from the temple."

"Those would be awesome to use against Plantera! Thanks!"

23

Plant Blender

I was in the dark jungle temple collecting super dart traps for the Plantera arena, and I needed to get in and out without dealing with the powerful lihzahrd enemies. I planned to collect wire and traps, and I needed to be careful because hitting one deadly trap would kill me. The traps would hopefully help me to kill Plantera. I spotted a lihzahrd coming toward me because I was trespassing in their temple deep in the jungle. I tried to hit the lihzahrd with my amarok yo-yo, but it escaped with barely a scratch! I encased the hallway in stone so the lihzahrd could not attack me. Then, I resumed searching the temple to find all of the super dart traps.

It took me weeks to safely find all of the traps in the jungle temple, but I finally completed my search. I just had to design a machine that would destroy Plantera, which gave me an idea. I planned to build a machine with traps and a teleporter to allow me to watch the fight in safety without dying from Plantera's devastating attacks. I had a chlorophyte crossbow to kill Plantera if something went wrong with my awesome plan.

I built a fort in the jungle and constructed a new arena underground around the Plantera bulb. I named my jungle fort Fort Antlion since I loved watching antlions spit sand at me. I built half of the Plantera killing machine, which used all of the diverse colors of wiring. I spent way too much gold on the expensive machine project, but I would rather be safe than sorry any day. I dug out the dirt around the Plantera bulb and had the bulb sitting on some floating dirt in the center of my arena. All of the traps pointed at the bulb so wherever Plantera moved, it would get hit. Plantera wouldn't be able to hit me because I would be teleporting around the arena. A hoik machine would have been better but more difficult to build. I finished the Plantera killing machine and planned to test it to make sure the wiring worked. Everything seemed okay so I turned the machine on, and it worked! Then, I placed a backup timer and left. I ate and rested so I could regain energy.

After a good rest, it was time to kill all of the enemies in the area and then break the Plantera bulb. I was at the top of the arena. I dug out of my camp to fill in the caves near the arena so nothing would spawn. It was hard work but worth it so I didn't have to deal with aggravating enemies spawning and attacking me while I was trying to defeat Plantera.

After I cleared the area, I was ready to smash the innocent looking bulb.

24

Bulb Bashing

I broke the bulb, and I ran to the teleporter nearest to me.

"Plantera has awoken."

I hit the button, but it didn't work! While making the backup timer, I had cut the wire, and I didn't have extra wire to fix my careless mistake! Plantera's pointy hook grabbed onto the wall beside me. Backup plan! I had to use the crossbow and chlorophyte claymore to kill Plantera's hook. I suddenly stopped liking plants.

I had a good supply of arrows; therefore, I thought I had enough to kill Plantera. No I didn't! I only had one hundred arrows, and I needed more than three hundred to even have a chance of denting Plantera's health! I decided to use some of the arrows and then use all of my close range melee weapons to hopefully keep me alive. Things were not looking good. I summoned my baby face monster pet to distract Plantera because face monsters have the loudest screams ever known. It worked! Every time my baby face monster screamed, Plantera stayed still for two seconds because it was confused about who it was supposed to attack! At that point, I decided I could possibly survive! Oh no, my pet baby face monster had stopped screaming. That was not good. Then it was just me and Plantera. I used the rest of my arrows except one single ichor arrow, and Plantera was only at three fourths health. I needed to use the chlorophyte claymore. Plantera was shooting seeds at high velocity at me, and they hurt. I ran under Plantera to kill the hooks. They didn't have much health so it was relatively easy to kill the hooks except for the fact that I was being chased by a psycho plant that shot seeds. The only option I had left to try was to hit Plantera when it was vulnerable and run when it was not. Plantera kept getting more angry, and it kept getting faster. If not for my lightning boots, which I spent hours crafting, I would have been dead.

I hoped the battle wouldn't go on much longer because I was getting tired. Luckily, Plantera was at half health. Oh no! Plantera had gone crazy. It was zooming at me and trying to eat me. Plantera bit my leg, which made a sickening crack. Fortunately, I used a sword to support my broken leg so I could continue the fight. Plantera was at the top of the arena. It turned and dove to the bottom of the arena on top of me. It nearly bit my head off!

Plantera went for the kill. How could any boss be more difficult than the monstrosity I currently faced? I didn't understand how the guide thought there were bosses more difficult than Plantera. I wondered if I would make it! I wished I was able to respawn. That would have been really nice. Unfortunately, I had to deal with a biological threat to humanity. How could it get any worse? I shouldn't have said that! Plantera was as fast as my lightning boots. If it got any faster, I would surely die! I had to fly away from Plantera after each strike so it wouldn't bite me. Plantera was catching up! I needed to move faster. But how? Flying was the only answer, but my wings were barely able to stay ahead of Plantera. I needed to kill it quickly, or I wouldn't even make it out of the battle alive.

I was just about to hit Plantera from behind, but Plantera stopped and turned to face me. I couldn't stop myself from flying into its mouth, and Plantera bit my arm. My arm snapped, but Plantera just kept going. My suspicions about not making it out of the battle alive were coming true. I stopped and immediately turned to confuse Plantera about where I would strike next. Plantera stopped and turned too since I was not in its line of destruction anymore. I turned again to use my sword to hack at its body. Plantera tried to bite me, but I ran to its backside. I hit it a couple of times then ran. Plantera quickly resumed the chase. Plantera was at one quarter health. I only had a little left to go! I wondered if I could use the backup timer to power the machine. Why hadn't I thought of that sooner?

I ran to the switch and pressed the button to activate. It didn't make the teleporters work, but the traps worked! Oh wow! I was so smart. I would have to run through spike traps and get impaled by spears. I turned the broken machine off. Plantera was barely alive. I put my single remaining arrow in the crossbow. Oh no! Plantera was about to swallow me whole. That was it. The end of my journey. I shot one last time. Boom! The arrow went down Plantera's throat and exploded deep inside the green scary plant! Plantera fell dead before me. Wow! I had barely survived the battle with Plantera!

25

Stony Battle

It took a few short months after my battle with Plantera until I felt restored and ready to fight again! During my recovery, I crafted a cell phone because I knew it would come in handy. I placed a lihzahrd alter in the same jungle arena where I fought Plantera, and I also crafted frostspark boots for maximum speed. I finally had an ankh shield. It took months to pick up all of the recipe to make the legendary ankh shield. I was prepared to fight Golem! All I needed to do was use the power cell I had found in a lihzahrd chest in the jungle temple!

"Golem has awoken."

It was always so weird when the creepy voice spoke. Oh wow! Golem was made completely of stone. It was a giant, stone juggernaut! I immediately thought up a litany of ways the battle could go wrong. I awoke from my thoughts and narrowly dodged a giant fist that flew from

Golem like a spring. It was going to be a tough battle, but all I had to do was destroy the fists and head and then the body. I dropped Golem's fist to half health. My chlorophyte claymore saved me time and time again. It was a great melee backup weapon because it did high damage and shot a projectile that could travel a moderate distance. I had gone to the goblin tinkerer to upgrade it to an unreal chlorophyte claymore for more damage. I was wearing my set of turtle armor so I reflected damage back to Golem, who was getting a taste of its own medicine! Its fists were deadly, and I couldn't afford to get hit. If I needed to escape, I had a shaft that went to the surface of the jungle. I chopped through one of Golem's fists, and it fell to the ground. Golem was useless on its left side without a fist. I had just one more fist to go! Oof! Golem spun and its right fist smashed me into the wall. Golem made a powerful punch again, but I dodged the deadly blow and grabbed its fist. I kept stabbing the fist with the shadow flame dagger I carried in my belt. The fist dropped to quarter health then fell to the floor. I grabbed the repeater I carried and started shooting Golem's head.

I wasn't paying attention to anything else, and I forgot that Golem could smash me with its feet. Thud! I got pushed into the mud by Golem's heavy stone foot. I kept getting stomped down with Golem's feet, and I was suffocating in the dirt. I pulled out the rod of discord, which had dropped from a hallow enemy, and teleported onto Golem's head. I pointed my repeater down at Golem's head and let the arrows fly. When I finally destroyed the head, I got launched into the air by the force of the blast. The pieces of Golem's head suddenly merged back together, started shooting lasers and flew around above Golem's body. I needed to destroy the chest to win the battle against Golem!

Many yellow lasers streaked toward me, and I couldn't dodge them fast enough. One hit my shoulder, and my arm snapped and hung limp by my side. I needed to kill Golem's body, or I would get turned into a pancake. I kept dodging the lasers! Ouch! A laser barely skimmed my arm but still made welts appear around the cut. It was time to switch to Plan B! I had gone into the dungeon a while ago, and I had a paladin's hammer! Pow! Pow! It worked! Golem was almost dead, and stone was falling from its body. I struck Golem's chest with all of my might, and Golem fell dead at my feet as its head flew away.

26

Chopping with Hatchet

After my battle with Golem, I finally had the possessed hatchet, which automatically locked onto my enemies and killed them! I needed to use the beetle shells that dropped from Golem and find more turtle shells to craft a full set of the amazing beetle armor. It had very high defense and would be incredibly useful in the upcoming boss fights. Using the possessed hatchet, which dealt high damage, it was going to be easy to gather the valuable turtle shells in the jungle.

I traveled to the jungle, and I spotted some giant tortoises with my binoculars. As I ran closer, they started spinning through the air toward me. I waited until they were in range before I threw the possessed hatchet. They all split and fell to the ground dead. That hatchet really worked!

I traveled back to the village and combined my

turtle armor with the beetle shells to craft beetle armor. I decided it was time to prepare to fight Duke Fishron! I needed some more supplies, and then I would be ready for the excruciating battle. I had all of the items I needed to craft ninja gear, which would help me dodge, dash and climb in the battle against Duke Fishron. The ninja gear was so cool!

I planned to buy a Hercules beetle from the witch doctor.

"What does thee want?" asked the witch doctor in his creepy voice.

"I want a Hercules beetle."

"Give me forty gold."

"Here, I put in five more for a tip."

"Here you go, and be careful with it."

The witch doctor always creeped me out, but he was extremely useful.

I also visited the steampunker and bought a pair of steampunk wings, which would help me fly higher for boss fights. I thought I was invincible! Alpha the Cyborg moved in and sold useful items like a mine launcher. I held a feast with all of the villagers to celebrate!

"This party needs confetti," said the party girl.

"Well, enjoy the party since it took a while to plan."

"Eric, what is that thing over there?" asked the

party girl as she pointed in the distance.

I looked in my binoculars and saw a little green thing over the hill. "It looks like a slime, but it is too far away to tell."

"It's a Martian probe!" said Aiden, the arms dealer.

"You believe in that myth?" asked the demolitionist.

"Guys, I didn't know slimes can fly," I worriedly said.

"One slime can, but it is purple and only appears in the corruption. It has to be a Martian probe!" said Aiden. He pulled out a minishark gun and loaded it with silver bullets. As the object flew closer to the village, the demolitionist pulled out some grenades.

"It is a Martian probe!" I shouted. "The Martians are invading!"

27

Space Invasion

Hundreds of ugly Martians spawned and were marching toward us. Aiden was the only one who was prepared for their invasion, and he stepped outside and started shooting the Martian engineers and tesla turrets with his minishark gun. I ran out to help Aiden, but the Martians were approaching too quickly. Aiden got shot by a ray gunner and fell into a bloody heap on the ground. Alpha used a rocket launcher, which fired rocket IVs at the Martians. The rockets blew holes in the ground. The clothier's house blew up when a Martian drone kamikazed into it. Martian officers put up shields and blew up houses. Aiden got up and tried to shoot another tesla turret. He destroyed it, but another one blasted Aiden, and he fell down again. I used the possessed hatchet to shred some of the gray grunts, but there were just too many.

"Bombs away!" yelled the demolitionist.

I immediately grabbed Aiden and flew up into the air to safety. Below us, I could see a swarm of Martians. Booooom! At the edge of the village, the demolitionist detonated a huge chunk of buried dynamite. The Martian ranks were decimated, and all of the villagers cheered. A huge Martian saucer approached in the distance. A spray of lasers destroyed the landscape, and the saucer launched a death ray, which left a crater in the ground. The saucer also fired missiles, and one missile locked onto me. I landed and ran into a large stone bunker with Aiden. I couldn't close the door fast enough, and the missile followed me in. All of the furniture blew up, and the fiery debris sprayed across the bunker, which shook but held up.

I cracked the door and peaked out. The villagers were mostly gone. Nurse Kelly and Alpha were trapped in a house across the street, which had started to shake as the Martians continued to fire upon it. Tesla turrets were everywhere. I opened up a small hole in the roof of the bunker and used my trusted kraken to destroy the Martian saucer's cannons and turrets. The Martian saucer shot another death ray that completely demolished most of the remaining houses in the village. I used a megashark gun, which blew up the saucer, and then I tunneled under the fallen houses to Kelly and Alpha. I grabbed them and covered the exit.

The Martians finally figured out how to open a non-holographic doorknob and were able to enter the last buildings that remained standing. They kept shooting at the last house, and it finally collapsed, killing a few gray grunts inside. I had forgotten I could use the possessed hatchet in a small opening! I grabbed my hatchet and threw it outside. It flew through the air, shredding the Martians, but there were too many of them. I needed something new. I wondered if the charged blaster cannon that had dropped from the Martian saucer would work. We ran through a small mine, which opened out onto the top of the hill.

I stood on the hill and fired the charged blaster cannon, and an orb of light disintegrated a Martian engineer. It was awesome! I waited to get a full charge. Zap! A solid beam vaporized most of the remaining Martians in the village. Aiden, Kelly and Alpha cheered. I waited to hear more cheers. My wings faltered in the air as I realized that there were only three villagers left. I launched more beams at the few Martians remaining. I wanted them dead.

I noticed some wood planks move. The painter was alive! I raced toward him, and I reached out to grab him. Suddenly, a missile hit the painter, and he disintegrated. I was thrown backward into the dirt. I couldn't reach my pickaxe, and I was stuck! Lasers landed around me. I wiggled until my wings could lift me out. As I emerged from the dirt, I came face to face with a Martian drone. It flew closer to me, and I shot it with my venus magnum gun. Another Martian saucer flew toward me, and I shot it with a solid beam of energy from the charged blaster cannon. Its cannons and turrets died, and it was blasted to quarter health before I ran out of mana. My possessed hatchet took care of the rest. The saucer dropped a ufo car key, which would allow me to fly indefinitely through the air! I used my new ufo mount to fly over to Aiden, Kelly and Alpha on the hill.

"Did the painter survive the hit?" I asked.

"No, he was too far beyond repair," Nurse Kelly responded.

I used the charged blaster cannon again, and a beam of energy destroyed a scutlix, which dropped a brain scrambler. Another Martian saucer arrived. I flew around it while shooting orbs of energy. It flew above me and launched a death ray at me. I was pushed toward the ground, and my ufo mount broke and fell into pieces. I used the charged blaster cannon to kill the Martian saucer, and it dropped an influx waver, which was by far my best weapon.

"The Martians are defeated."

Whew, that was difficult!

28

Fishing

Over time, the villagers respawned and eventually every house was filled again. I went to visit the guide.

"I'm ready to move on to the next bosses. What weapon do I need?"

"The possessed hatchet will work well in a battle with Duke Fishron, but the flairon will be the best weapon to use after you defeat Duke Fishron," the guide said.

"Thank you."

I was ready to fight Duke Fishron and get the legendary flairon, which I needed to kill the next bosses. My possessed hatchet just wouldn't cut it because it needed more damage per second to be a good weapon to use in fighting more powerful bosses. I needed a weapon capable of accurate homing, high damage, high speed, and high damage per second. I wanted the flairon because it was fast and shot out homing projectiles that dealt high damage. I finished rebuilding the village before I left to find the rare truffle worm to use as the bait for Duke Fishron.

After two hours of bug searching, I finally found a blue truffle worm in a glowing mushroom biome. I only had one worm so I needed to kill Duke Fishron and get a flairon on my first try. I had repaired my ufo mount so I could fly indefinitely, which was about the most useful item I had in my supplies. I traveled to the arena near Fort Terra beside the ocean. I chopped a tree and crafted a simple fishing rod. I threw my line into the water and waited.

"Duke Fishron has awoken."

A mutant pigron/fish flew out of the water and barreled toward me. I dodged its first attack. I was really glad the possessed hatchet had precise homing! I used my hatchet to slash Duke Fishron twice in the gills. Duke Fishron summoned a sharknado, which shot high speed vicious sharks at me. Toxic bubbles flew after me as I tried to dodge the attacks. Duke Fishron hit me and bulldozed me like a rag doll over onto a platform. Sharks started hitting me from every direction because of the sharknados. I chugged a healing potion that I had brewed at the alchemy table I found in the dungeon. I couldn't drink more than one because the healing potion made me sick for a few hours as a side effect. I jumped over a shark as bubbles were chasing me, but my possessed hatchet sliced them up easily so I could focus solely on Duke Fishron. I dodged Duke Fishron's charge and hit one of its fins. Duke Fishron started spinning faster and faster in a wheel of death. Duke Fishron had reached its second phase!

Duke Fishron flew at me at speeds greater than I had ever seen from any other boss. I got hit and spun into the air. Duke Fishron teleported beside me and hit me again. I used my grappling hook to bring myself back to the ground far below me, and I jumped over Duke Fishron as he teleported underneath me. I threw my possessed hatchet and used its homing to strike Duke Fishron in the gills again. It became faster the more I damaged it. I got hit out of nowhere, only to see Duke Fishron teleport behind me. I stopped using my ufo mount because it didn't slow down, turn, or move fast enough. I used my beetle wings to gain the extra speed, which was crucial. Duke Fishron was at quarter health and was constantly teleporting. Without my homing, I wouldn't have known where it was. Duke Fishron hit my wings and snapped them into two pieces. I was left with no way to dodge the attacks! I was rammed twice, causing me to hit the ground at an odd angle. I threw my possessed hatchet at Duke Fishron's face just as he was about to hit me again. Duke Fishron split in two and fell to the ground.

"Duke Fishron has been defeated."

29

Ultimate Weapon

I drank a greater healing potion and looked down. I saw the flairon I so desperately needed near my feet! I picked it up and swung it at an angry shark. Bubbles came out and destroyed the shark instantly. I could get used to that! The flairon was the ultimate homing weapon, which would dish out massive damage in a second. The guide really knew his stuff about good and bad weapons. The flairon was definitely the weapon I would use to fight the upcoming bosses.

I used my informative cell phone, which I had crafted during my spare time recovering from Plantera's battle, and teleported back to the village. As I walked through the village to visit the helpful guide, the villagers congratulated me and wished me luck with the next bosses I would encounter. The villagers had a sad look in their eyes like it would be the last time they would ever see me.

The guide pulled me into his mahogany house.

"Eric, the next boss is the Lunatic Cultist. He will be twenty times as hard as Duke Fishron. After you kill it, the lunar event will start and after that...," The guide looked down and studied the floor.

"What?"

"Nothing. You'll be fine."

"Are you sure?"

"Yes, I'll get you some greater healing potions, and then you can be on your way."

The guide hurried out, and I wondered what was making everyone so anxious. He came back with his arms full of the potions that the wizard had created while I was away.

"Here you go! That should be all! The party girl has planned a huge party to celebrate, and it starts at seven. Then you can sleep and be on your way," the guide said.

I had fun at the party. We talked about my Duke Fishron battle. Apparently, there had been a shockwave from the sharknados that blew some of the village fences down. The guide took notes about how Duke Fishron behaved for future reference. After the meal, I returned to my house and sat down on my bed. I thought of the villagers and the sad looks they had given me. I stayed awake and wondered what could be so bad to make them look at me that way, and I eventually fell asleep.

I woke up the next morning and said goodbye to the villagers. Then, I was on my way to the dungeon, which took only a day with my amazing ufo mount. I didn't know how I had ever survived with the limited flight bee mount. It was a nice ride. I just sat on it, and my optic staff's minions took care of everything. It was an easy trip. I didn't encounter anything that my minions couldn't handle, just an occasional herpling or pixie. I arrived at the dungeon just as it turned night. According to the guide, nighttime was the time I should fight the Lunatic Cultist. I charged his followers, and my flairon tore through them.

"The Lunatic Cultist has awoken."

30

Fighting a Psycho

The Lunatic Cultist rose above me and started chanting its mysterious language. I used the flairon to deal massive damage. I learned that I should not hit an enemy directly with the flairon's head but instead hit close to the enemy to release the maximum bubbles to home in on the enemy. Instead of having around five bubbles when I hit an enemy directly with the flairon's head, I would have thirteen bubbles that homed in, dealing over one thousand damage! The Lunatic Cultist teleported higher above me and started attacking. It made an ice ball that spun sharp spikes out. One barely missed me and hit the dungeon wall. I was glad the ice spikes weren't homing. The Lunatic Cultist then made fireballs that homed in on me. One hit my shoulder, and my ufo mount spun around. I couldn't take a direct hit on my ufo mount, or it might malfunction and drop to the ground in pieces! The Lunatic Cultist summoned a glowing orb that shot out lightning bolts at me. I kept dealing massive damage with my flairon. The Lunatic Cultist duplicated twice, and the three Lunatic Cultists formed a triangle in the air. I didn't know which one I should attack. One seemed more solid than the others, but I wasn't sure what that meant.

The triangle disappeared, and the three Lunatic Cultists flew around to different sides of me. I realized my mistake. I hadn't attacked the solid Lunatic Cultist in the triangle so the other two came to life! It was then that I realized I should always focus my attack on the solid one. The solid Lunatic Cultist made a giant dragon that smashed into my ufo mount. As the ufo's lights flickered off, it suddenly broke into pieces! As I was falling to the ground, I killed the Lunatic Cultist's dragon and then glided down using my wings. I dodged the eight ice spikes that the Lunatic Cultist fired at me. I hit it again and took it down to half health, but I suddenly flew through the air as an ice spike hit me from behind. I turned and saw the other two Lunatic Cultists! They were waiting for me to forget about them so they could surprise me. They launched the homing fireballs. I tried to dodge the fireballs, but one hit my wings as I flipped trying to dodge another. My wings looked stripped, but they could still fly.

All three Lunatic Cultists fired orbs that shot lightning bolts at me. I got hit by two bolts, which made my wings finally give out. I started free falling toward the dungeon's roof. In midair, I drank a healing potion that strengthened my wings enough to fly again. The Lunatic Cultists formed a pentagon shape in the air and did the same thing as last time but duplicated more cultists. While they were in the pentagon formation, I hit the solid one, and they all disappeared except the real one!

I smashed the Lunatic Cultist with one thousand damage again and again! I dodged all of the ice attacks it threw at me. A lightning bolt hit my wings, and I could only use my wings to glide down after that. I spotted a fireball coming at me so I stopped gliding and started freefalling to dodge the fireball by gaining speed. When I wasn't looking, the fireball turned using its homing and hit me in the back. The blast flipped me through the air, and my feet caught on the dungeon's roof, which made me jerk to a halt and face-plant into the roof. Another fireball hit my back and caused part of the dungeon's roof to collapse. I fell on the rubble, and it knocked the breath out of me. I stood up and hit the Lunatic Cultist again with my flairon. The rest of the dungeon's roof collapsed, and the ground started to shake. The Lunatic Cultist screamed and exploded. The explosion ripped the dungeon's remaining walls off and sent me flying hundreds of feet. Trees flew around me like someone was tossing them. I rammed into a hill, and the last thing I heard was…

"Celestial creatures are invading."

31

Eruption

I woke up as the sun started rising. I had been unconscious for hours! I stood up and looked around. I saw an ancient manipulator standing beside me. I picked it up because it would be useful later. As I continued looking around, I saw a giant pillar in the distance, and I wondered if it summoned the celestial creatures that were invading. I guessed that was what I needed to destroy next.

I reached the giant pillar in minutes with my repaired ufo mount. The sky turned a fiery red, and enemies started swarming me. I had never seen anything like it. I flew up into the red sky and killed the fiery enemies. A huge worm rammed me like a bullet train. I fell to the ground, and the worm circled above me. It must not have been able to fly near the ground. Almost instantly, I killed a fiery, flying lizard carrying a semi-human creature.

I got hit by a spinning ball that went through

blocks. It was an actual enemy that went through blocks! It charged me again, and I destroyed it. I flew up to dodge an attack from another dangerous enemy then killed the worm that had rammed me. I spun around to kill a powerful ice golem-like enemy, and I killed another worm that was circling above me. An enemy riding a lizard hit me with a spear, and I felt a searing pain in my side. I killed it and immediately drank a greater healing potion. Another spinning ball enemy hit me and ripped through my ufo mount, which flickered then broke. I killed the spinning ball enemy and used my wings to fly over another lizard. I killed it and fell on a celestial creature.

I suddenly remembered that my cell phone would tell me what the creatures were named! The spinning thing was a corite; the golem thing, a sroller; the worm, a crawltipede; the javelin thrower, a drakanian; the enemy with knives, a selenian; and the lizard, a drakomire. Another drakanian threw a spear at me. I flew over it and killed the drakanian and crawltipede simultaneously. I killed another drakanian and flew over to the pillar.

I tried to damage the pillar, but it was surrounded by a shield that I needed to disable. I killed a selenian and crawltipede. I jumped over a corite, only to run right into another. My leg felt like it was being ground up to dust. I looked down and saw that it was a bloody mess. It was the same leg that had been broken before. My new greater healing potions allowed me to heal wounds, which would have been very useful when I had broken my leg in the past. I could have avoided the long recovery process. I killed a sroller and a selenian. Suddenly, the pillar's shield went down.

I focused everything I had on killing the pillar. Enemies swarmed me. I tried to dodge and hit the enemies while attacking the pillar. I started taking hits more and more, and I realized I couldn't fight both at the same time. I needed to stop the enemies' source, which was the pillar. I stopped defending myself from enemies and focused solely on the pillar. I felt like a chew toy. A crawltipede rammed me, and I felt like I would die. I released one more hit from my flairon before my wings broke. The pillar and enemies exploded into light!

"Your mind goes numb."

Everything went black.

32

Stardust Battle

I woke up after a few hours, and I stood up and grabbed the celestial solar fragments. I placed my ancient manipulator down and crafted an eruption and daybreak, which were both very useful weapons, but I still liked the amazing flairon more because it had the needed homing and damage per second. I repaired my ufo mount and started flying.

After flying three hours, the sky turned blue, and I looked through my binoculars and saw another pillar looming in the distance. I flew toward it and started using my flairon. I easily smashed and killed a starry bubble-like enemy and broke it into five pieces. The tiny pieces didn't send their souls back to the pillar; I needed to let them regrow so more souls could return to the pillar, which would lower its shield. Two more enemy bubbles came at me. I chopped them and waited for them to regrow into their more powerful phase. I killed them again and let them regrow. Suddenly, I realized my mistake. Too many regrown enemies could quickly get out of hand, and they all swarmed me at once. I was knocked back and forth like a ping pong ball. I used my flairon, but I only took out five with every swing because the enemies were so close. My flairon lost its effectiveness when I couldn't release maximum homing bubbles to deal massive damage. The flairon was great for crowd control until you were completely surrounded by enemies, and there were sixty enemies at least!

A crab shot bullets at me. My ufo mount started to glide down. It couldn't take the brute force of ninety enemy bubbles against me. I glanced at my cell phone and discovered that the bubbles were star cells. A worm flew at me and completely wrecked my ufo mount. Lucky for me, that worm wasn't nearly as dangerous as the other solar type. I killed it and focused on the star cells. The crab was a twinkle popper, and the small bullet-sized ones were twinkles. They distracted me, and some star cells regrew. I fell to the ground, and I jumped up and shot the flairon into the air. I was far enough away from the enemies that the flairon's bubbles killed eight of the star cells, but that wasn't enough. I pulled out the eruption and swept into the star cells. Wow! The star cells took massive damage as it cut through at least twenty. I swept again to kill the rest.

I then used the flairon to kill the small ones. The eruption was a great crowd control weapon since there were so many enemies closely surrounding me. The flairon did well, but over fifty fast star cells with lots of health crowding around me made it inadequate. I killed another twinkle popper. A stargazer shot a powerful laser, knocking me to the ground, but I killed it very easily.

At that point, I wondered if I had killed enough enemies to lower the pillar's shield so I flew over to check on its status. It was enough! I switched to my flairon, and I started destroying the pillar. A worm hit me and spun me around. I killed it and figured out it was a milky way weaver. Another twinkle exploded against me. I killed the twinkle popper and swung at the pillar again.

I was knocked forward and smashed into the pillar, but I swung again to deliver another devastating blow. I pumped more and more hits into the pillar. The aggressive star cells threw me like a ping pong ball. I equipped my ankh shield, and it stopped the knock back! I easily killed the star cells and kept attacking the pillar. I finally destroyed it!

"You are overwhelmed with pain."

"Uh oh."

Everything went black…again.

33

Nebula Creator

After I woke up, I crafted a powerful stardust dragon staff, which summoned a crazy dragon that destroyed everything it touched! I easily flew to the next titanic pillar looming in the distance without any disruption because of my dragon. The sky turned purple, and I saw enemies approaching me. I used my cell phone to learn their names and entered the battle.

Three brain sucklers latched onto me, and I couldn't see! I killed them and wiped my armor clean. I killed a nebula floater just as it shot a laser at me. Its powerful laser created a deep cut in my leg armor, which left a vulnerable spot for me to get hit in the battle. An evolution beast ran at me. It was a psycho purple hound with big teeth, and it bit my leg and drug me around like a teddy bear. I hit it on the head, and the flairon's bubbles quickly finished the job. I killed a predictor before it could launch its attack. Predictors were very bad at predicting.

I killed another brain suckler as it tried to latch onto me. I felt like the brain sucklers were the most common enemy the third pillar summoned to attack me. A nebula floater shot a powerful bullet that fortunately didn't knock me back because of my useful ankh shield. My ufo mount was still holding up surprisingly well. I hit the nebula floater with one flairon bubble, but it teleported behind me and struck me again. I couldn't keep going! I wouldn't make it if I kept taking so much damage to my health. I aimed my flairon and hit the nebula floater. It teleported away, but the two flairon bubbles homed in on it. It didn't stand a chance. A brain suckler blocked my vision again while another predictor hit me with its powerful laser.

My ankh charm exploded, and I felt like I had been hit by a train. I flew through the air so fast that the brain suckler, which was latched onto me, couldn't hold on. I was moving at an insane speed that I had never reached before. I slammed into a nebula floater. My impact instantly killed it and stopped my flight through the air. It took me a few seconds to get back to the predictor and terminate it. An evolution beast bit a chunk out of my ufo mount, and then it spat out psycho nebula dog acid. The acid looked so deadly that I didn't want to know what happened if it touched me. I dodged the acid as it slowly homed in on me. The acid lost its homing and hit a tree, which immediately developed a gaping hole. The tree started to creak, and it broke and fell on the evolution beast. It had a bad day!

I killed a nebula floater with the influx waver, and then I switched back to my flairon and killed a predictor and an evolution beast. My next swing took out three brain sucklers. I tore through everything in my path because I had finished playing around! It was time to destroy the pillar. Five brain sucklers were split in two, thanks to my flairon. An evolution beast didn't even launch its spit before five flairon bubbles crashed into it. A predictor lined up to shoot me, but I swung twelve flairon bubbles that homed in on it. It still tried to get its shot, but it was too late. The predictor split into three purple pieces and fell to the ground. I pulled out my binoculars and looked at the pillar. Its shield was down! I flew at it, already swinging. At least twenty flairon bubbles hit it simultaneously. I swung at it again and again. A predictor shot its laser at me and knocked out my ufo mount. I started falling to the ground. On the way down, I swung at the predictor and killed it. I used my grappling hook for a close save, and I easily jumped off the mound of dirt. In one quick motion, I swung at the pillar, and it exploded into light.

"Otherworldly voices linger around you."

34

Vex of the Vortex

I grabbed the fragments and got up onto my ufo mount and flew off toward the final pillar. I wondered what would happen next. I let myself regain my health to be at maximum efficiency to be able to destroy the final pillar. I looked through my trusty binoculars. Nothing yet. All I could see was the dry desert dunes. A few minutes later, I looked again, and there it was!

I flew down and hurriedly researched the names of the enemies on my cell phone. The first enemy I met was a storm diver, but I killed it instantly. An alien queen attacked me with its stinger. I was unable to move up or down, and I was moving in a direct course to ram it. I smashed into the alien queen, and I killed the three larvae that spawned. I then killed an alien hornet before it could grow into a queen. I cut a storm diver open with my deadly flairon bubbles. A vortexian tried to punch my ufo, but he was in for a big surprise. What?! It punched right through my fragile ufo mount. I killed the vortexian and rose above the desert. I couldn't play games; the enemies were powerful and could easily kill me. I kept using the flairon and disintegrated another alien queen. After killing some larvae, I decided to get closer to the gigantic pillar.

I zoomed up to the pillar, but it still had its shield up. My flairon killed a few storm divers. An alien queen shot me again. I killed it, but I couldn't move up or down again. A storm diver shot my ankh shield, and my shield completely failed to stop the bullets from hitting my armor. I flipped off my ufo mount onto the dirt since my ankh shield had broken, and I jumped over another round of the deadly bullets. My flairon took out the storm diver and homed in on an alien hornet behind me. I tore through some larvae. They appeared everywhere! I cut through a storm diver and used my wings to dodge an alien hornet's stinger. I fired my flairon into the air, and it killed ten enemies around me. I kept giving the enemies a dose of my flairon's power. There were dead vortex enemies everywhere. I bet a dune splicer would have a great lunch feasting off all the dead enemies strewn about. A storm diver missed me, allowing me to kill it first. Enemy after enemy kept getting killed while trying to attack me. They couldn't attack me from behind because I was backed up against a stony hill, and none of them could pass through blocks. I killed another larva, and the pillar's impenetrable shield suddenly went down.

I focused all of my force into killing the pillar. I jumped over a larva and kept hitting the pillar. It dropped to half health, but that wasn't good enough. I hit it again. A vortexian behind me clawed my armor to shreds, and I summoned my stardust dragon to kill the vortexian so I could focus on the pillar. Suddenly, the pillar faded into light, and I heard screaming before everything went silent.

"Impending doom approaches."

35

The Final Battle!

The desert rumbled, and I saw a flock of vultures fleeing. I had made it to the final battle. I cleared out some space and got my potions ready. Ironskin, wrath, and a sharpening station. I summoned my dragon and repaired my ufo mount and ankh shield. I was ready for the final boss.

"The Moon Lord has awoken!"

A mutant monster bigger than anything I had ever seen rose out of the ground. It had an eye on each of its hands. I was ready. I dodged phantasmal eyes coming out of its hands, and I swung at them with all of my strength. I planned to take both hands out at the same time. I swung again and again, but I barely damaged them. The hands had over thirty thousand health each! Phantasmal spheres appeared around me. They didn't move but exploded at me, and I was moderately hurt by their sudden explosions.

The left hand's eye opened, and I hit it with nine hundred damage from my flairon. I rushed forward to dodge more homing phantasmal eyes.

The Moon Lord's top eye opened and started to summon a beam. I tried to go above it, but I was too late. The Moon Lord's huge beam cut ravines through the ground. The beam hit me, and I felt like I had been hit by every boss at once. I hit the Moon Lord's top eye twice before it closed. It felt like my insides had been hit with dynamite. My ufo mount barely held up against the powerful blast of phantasmal energy. I drank a greater healing potion and resumed the fight. I hit the gigantic left eye, and I dodged the phantasmal spheres that exploded. I zoomed down under the phantasmal eyes to hit the left eye again. I let my trusty stardust dragon hit the right eye to deal extra damage.

As I focused on the left eye, the Moon Lord's mouth opened and stuck a leach tentacle on me. It sucked my life force toward the Moon Lord's mouth. I destroyed the energy as it approached the Moon Lord's mouth, and the leach went back inside. Phantasmal bolts homed in on me as the Moon Lord opened its top eye once again. One phantasmal bolt hit me, but luckily it didn't do much harm to me or my ufo mount. I flew above the Moon Lord's eye to avoid the death ray. The Moon Lord was following me through the sky, and it was just a bit slower than my ufo mount. Another ravine appeared where its death ray landed. I hit the Moon Lord's top eye with five more destructive hits before it closed.

I returned my attention back to the left eye and swung at it. I flew over a few phantasmal eyes that homed in on me. I continued hitting the left eye until it was nearly dead. I flew over to the Moon Lord's right hand because I had planned to take both the left and right eyes out at the same time. The phantasmal spheres hit me once and made my ufo mount spin a little off course into a phantasmal bolt. My flairon slammed into the right eye and made a devastating blow to the gigantic eye. It took several minutes to even dent the health of the seemingly invincible monstrosities. I smashed the right eye with another high damage blow. The Moon Lord's top eye opened and fired its sweeping beam of destruction. I flew above the Moon Lord to get around the death ray, which cut a mountain in two. I took the top eye down to half health before it closed once again. I needed to attack the top eye about two more times to destroy it.

I focused on the right eye again. I got hit by a phantasmal eye then by a bolt. Fortunately, they didn't do very much damage to my health as they both dealt very low damage. The Moon Lord's mouth opened and stuck the leach tentacle on me again. I killed the glowing energy so the Moon Lord couldn't heal itself, and the tentacle went back into its mouth. The last thing I needed was for the Moon Lord to heal itself back to full health! As I continued fighting the right eye, I dodged another small bolt that came from the left eye. The Moon Lord opened its top eye and started to charge up to shoot the destructive beam. I flew up above its head to dodge the fatal attack, and I hit the top eye again before it closed. I remembered my dragon and whistled to it, signaling it to make the top eye its highest priority. I returned to my attack of the right eye and got smashed by a phantasmal sphere from behind. The leach tentacle attached to me again. I flew up then made a dive down to dodge a phantasmal eye. I killed more energy traveling up the tentacle. The Moon Lord's top eye opened again, but before it could fire, I killed it. The top eye popped out and started attacking me.

I immediately killed the right and left eyes before they could launch the phantasmal eyes. Three true Eyes of Cthulhu popped out and started attacking. The cover on the Moon Lord's heart split and opened up. I dodged the phantasmal bolts and eyes from the true Eyes of Cthulhu. With my dragon alongside me, I hit the heart more and more.

The eyes launched out mini death rays, which didn't do nearly as much damage as the Moon Lord's phantasmal death ray. I heard a few trees fall because of the mini death rays. I got hit by all three mini death rays because I wasn't quick enough to dodge them. I hit the heart again and started gliding down because I had nearly made it to space! I went into a slow dive going left to right to try to dodge some of the homing projectiles, and then I swooped up to avoid hitting the desert dunes. I got hit by two more mini death rays because I couldn't avoid them, but the true Eyes of Cthulhu's bolts couldn't hit me as I swept back and forth trying to dodge the phantasmal eyes and bolts. I hit the heart and got it to half health. I was nearly there! I hit a true Eye of Cthulhu and spun out of control as ten bolts smashed into me.

As I started to regain control of the ufo mount, I got hit by all three of the death rays. My ufo mount started descending uncontrollably again. It was going to be close. I couldn't stop the descent because my ufo mount had only survived because of the earlier healing potion. Since I had already drank one, I couldn't drink another, or I would lose consciousness. I was trying everything I could think of to stop the descent. I finally drank a regeneration potion, which stopped the descent as another death ray hit me.

I started loosing elevation again as my ufo mount could not sustain its height in the air because of the high damage it had taken. I was desperate for something to stop the ufo mount's fall. Another death ray hit my ufo mount, and all hope of fixing it was lost. I jumped out and used my wings to fly safely to the ground. I flew up and struck the heart again and flew in circles to avoid being hit by the death rays. Luckily, I dodged all three. I had to glide down since my wings would not fly forever. I landed and immediately jumped back up into the fight. Three phantasmal eyes hit my wings, and I fell to the hard ground. I stood up and gave another swing, and the Moon Lord rose above me and started exploding into light.

"The Moon Lord has been defeated!"

I picked up the hearts to regenerate some of my health, and I picked up a terrarian yo-yo. I swung it, and it stayed out indefinitely. It launched homing projectiles too! It was the ultimate upgraded flairon! I sat down on the dune and looked at the huge ravines created from the Moon Lord's eyes. I picked up the luminite and headed back home.

When I reached the village, I crafted solar armor and wings. I showed the villagers the Moon Lord's loot, and of course the party girl suggested we have a celebration. We talked about the fight and how the terrarian yo-yo was such an awesome weapon. The villagers could see where the final battle took place from the top of the village's tallest buildings.

As time passed, I kept exploring and fighting, but I was never challenged again.

Rate and Review

IMPORTANT - The most important thing you can do for an author is to leave a review of their work. Good or bad, it is important. Please take the time to leave a review on Amazon.com or GoodReads. It would mean a lot to me.